Ottie Slockett

Ottie Slockett

by Ida Luttrell
pictures by Ute Krause

Dial easy-to-read

Dial Books for Young Readers · New York

Published by Dial Books for Young Readers
A Division of Penguin Books USA Inc.
375 Hudson Street
New York, New York 10014

Published simultaneously in Canada by
Fitzhenry & Whiteside Limited, Toronto
Text copyright © 1990 by Ida Luttrell
Pictures copyright © 1990 by Ute Krause
Printed in Hong Kong by
South China Printing Company (1988) Limited
The Dial Easy-to-Read logo is a registered trademark of
Dial Books for Young Readers,
a division of Penguin Books USA Inc., ® TM 1,162,718.

Library of Congress Cataloging in Publication Data
Ottie Slockett / by Ida Luttrell; illustrated by Ute Krause.
p. cm.
Summary: Ottie Slockett finally learns that the way
to be friends with his neighbors is not to be a meddler.
ISBN 0-8037-0709-6 ISBN 0-8037-0711-8 (lib. bdg.)
[1. Friendship—Fiction. 2. Behavior—Fiction.
3. Neighborliness—Fiction.] I. Krause, Ute, ill.
II. Title. III. Series.
PZ7.L979530t 1990 [E]—dc19 88-30884 CIP AC

First Edition
W
1 3 5 7 9 10 8 6 4 2

The artwork for each picture consists of a black ink
and watercolor painting, which is camera-separated
and reproduced in full color.

Reading Level 2.1

To Lisa, Courtney, and Gregory
I.L.

To Chris and K.
U.K.

Ottie Slockett did not have

a cat or a dog or anyone to care

if he came or went.

So he moved to a busy street

in the city and tried to find something

to fill the empty place inside him.

Ottie looked out the window
at the front of his house.
He saw birds everywhere.
He also saw Mr. Stern's
house across the street.

8

Mr. Stern was resting
in his hammock.
The grass in his yard
was very tall.

"Oh, my," said Ottie, and he
ran across the street.

"You need to cut your grass,"
Ottie said.

"You don't say," said Mr. Stern.
And he closed his eyes,
pulled down his cap,
and went to sleep.

Ottie went home and looked out
the back window. He saw Mrs. Snow
hanging clothes on the line.
Her cat was on the roof.

"Uh, oh," said Ottie.

He picked up the phone
and called Mrs. Snow.

"Your cat is out," he said.

"Imagine that," said Mrs. Snow.

She hung up the phone
and went back
to her clothesline.

Ottie felt very helpful. He looked out
the window on the side of his house.
He saw Mrs. Pepper walking her dog.
"Good grief," said Ottie.
He ran outside.

"You need to go on a diet," he said.

"Is that so!" said Mrs. Pepper.

And she went in her house

and slammed the door so hard,

it scared the birds.

Ottie started home.

Two girls were jumping rope

on the sidewalk.

"All that jumping will shake
your brains loose," Ottie said.
"It will not," said Karen.
But she stopped jumping.
Lucy stopped jumping too
and felt her head.

Ottie went inside his house
and back to his windows.
The more Ottie watched,
the better he liked watching.

"I wish I could see more neighbors,"
he said to himself.
"But my windows are too small."
So Ottie made all his windows bigger.

Now he could see more houses
and he had more people to call.
Ottie kept busy watching and calling.

But his neighbors were tired of Ottie.

Mr. Stern would not come out
of his house.

Mrs. Snow put a pillow
over her phone,

and Mrs. Pepper walked her dog

after dark.

Ottie's empty feeling grew.

Hmph! Ottie thought,

What a bunch of stuck-up people.

Not one hello or thank you

for all my trouble.

I will find other houses to watch.

Ottie took out all of his windows

and put in glass walls.

When he finished,

it was time to go to bed.

24

Ottie was very happy
with his little glass house.
The next morning he dressed
quickly and ate his breakfast.
Then he ran to his front wall.
He could see every bird in every
tree and every house on the block.
"Aha," he said, and rushed
to the phone.

Before he could reach it
the phone rang.

Mr. Stern was calling.

"You forgot to make your bed,"
he said.

"You don't say," said Ottie.

26

The phone rang again.

"You did not wash behind your ears,"
said Mrs. Pepper.

Ottie's dirty ears turned red.

"Is that so!" he said.

He put the phone down.

It rang again.

"You left your dishes

in the sink," said Mrs. Snow.

"Imagine that!" said Ottie.

The phone rang all day.

Everyone up and down the street

called Ottie.

They told him how to brush

his teeth and comb his hair

and mend his socks and underwear.

Ottie threw his phone out the door.

"Meddlers!" he yelled.

And the word rang in his ears.

Ottie went to work hanging sheets
across his glass walls.

But that word would not go away.

Me, a meddler? Ottie thought.

And it kept him awake all night.

The next day Ottie went for a walk
and tried not to meddle.

Mr. Stern was polishing his car.

Ottie wanted to say,

"That is the wrong kind of wax."

But he said, "You have a nice car."

"Thanks," said Mr. Stern,

and he smiled.

Ottie saw Lucy taking her turn
at hopscotch while Karen
pushed a doll-buggy full of puppies.

Ottie did not tell them "Hopping

will crack the bones in your feet"

or "You will make those puppies sick,"

even if that is what he was thinking.

He said, "Having fun?"

Lucy and Karen grinned.

"Yes," they said.

Soon it became easy for Ottie to smile
and say "Hello" or "Good day,"
instead of "Are you wearing a wig?"
or "Have you been in a fight?"
or "Did your dress shrink?"

Before long Mr. Stern invited Ottie
to play cards.
Mrs. Snow took him to a ball game,
and Mrs. Pepper baked a pie for him.

Karen and Lucy gave him a puppy.
It wagged when Ottie came home
and cried when he left.
And Ottie's empty feeling went away.

No matter how hard he tried though,
Ottie could not give up watching.

But the birds didn't care.